CW00862721

The Magic Storybook For Amazing Girls

Inspiring Tales For Girls That Bring Adventures to Life

MARK CHAPEL

Copyright © [2022] [Mark Chapel]

All rights reserved

All rights for this book here presented belong exclusively to the author.

Usage or reproduction of the text is forbidden and requires a clear consent of the author in case of expectations.

ISBN - 9798812242114

THE BOOK BELONGS TO

··

··

✳ 4 ✳

Table of Contents

The Magic Story Book for Amazing Girls.

Remember when you were young? What were the best stories? That's right, the ones that are steeped in magic and wonder. Just look at the tales and stories that we find today in our films, television, and books. These types of stories seem more popular now than ever. Such stories have been with us for a very long time.

Stories and tales of far-off lands that come filled with promises. Stories of fantastical characters, daring action, suspense, and thrilling tales of daring deeds and derring-do.

Why are we so drawn to the fantastic in our stories? Because that's what stories are for. Stories are where we go to escape. Everybody deserves some time out from the familiarity of the everyday.

So, please come in, pull up a chair, the tale is about to begin. Some might be funny, some might be sad, some might even be a little bit scary, as that can be fun as well. Every hero needs a cunning adversary after all... Wicked queens abound in the land of far, far away.

Twice upon a once or once upon a time. The possibilities are endless.

The Frogs and the Farmer.

Ponds can be the most beautiful of things. You can find them in many gardens and you can see them when exploring the countryside. Ponds support all kinds of life. In your average pond you can find water snails, beetles, dragonflies, damsel flies, waterlilies, water violets, newts, minnow fish, and, most common of all, frogs.

The pond in our story is inhabited by a family of brightest green frogs. Mother Felicity and Father Finlay were parents to three younger frogs, two girls and a boy, named Fifi, Florence and Felix. Of course, they all had the surname Frog. For that's often how surnames work.

The Frogs lived a happy and idyllic life in their pond. Sometimes children would visit and feed them chickweed, which was a particular favourite of theirs. Their pond was quite beautiful and undisturbed by the city, which was many miles away. The family would spend many a happy summers day catching flies, holding swimming races, or just floating wrong-side up and having their bellies warmed by the glorious sunshine.

All was well and good until one month a city farmer and his wife decided to pack up their business, move to the countryside, and buy the field in which our Frog pond was found. The farmer and his wife were known as Mr and Mrs Jethroe. They had a plan to grow a large field of wheat in the grassy meadow where we find our family.

As a businessman and farmer Mr Jethroe had one priority in life. His main aim was to make as much money as possible from the land that he owned. On surveying the beautiful meadow Mr Jethroe had an idea, and it was an idea that would mean very bad news for Felicity, Finlay and their children.

The Frog pond was fed by a small stream. Mr Jethroe decided that he could grow more wheat if he blocked up this stream, dried out the pond, and planted seeds where it was situated. That very same day he got in his tractor and dumped some haybales into the stream creating a dam. The Frog family felt the effects of this immediately. In no time at all the pond began to dry out.

Felicity, alarmed, went to speak to her husband, "Finlay! What are we to do? If the pond dries out, we'll have to leave this meadow and find a new home for our children. If we can't find a home before winter we shall surely perish."

Finlay reassured his wife that she should not panic. Since the farmer and his wife had moved into the area, he had made friends with some of their animals. And with that he hopped off to have a word Gracie the Goat.

"Hello Gracie. I hope you're feeling well on this fine summer day. I was wondering if you could help me with a bit of a problem myself and my family are having." Finlay explained the situation with the haybales. Together they set off to the part of the stream where they were creating a dam.

Gracie was a huge fan of hay; she could happily munch it all day. In no time at all she had eaten a large enough hole in the haybales. The water from the stream was once again running freely. Finlay Frog thanked her very much and returned home to find a much-relieved Felicity Frog and Family.

On finding this the next day Mr Jethroe was furious. He got back in his tractor. This time he filled the trailer with a large mound of mud. Once again, he dumped this mud into the stream and created another dam. "I can't see any of my animals wanting to eat mud. That should sort it!"

Immediately, back at the pond, things began to dry up around the Frogs. "It's happening again Finlay!" Felicity cried.

"Don't worry Felicity. I know just the friend who can sort this out for us." And with that he hopped off to have a word with Pandora the Pig.

"Hello Pandora. I hope you're feeling well on this fine summer day. I was wondering if you could help me with a bit of a problem me and my family are having?" Once again, they set off to where the stream had been blocked. This time by the big mound of mud. There was little more in the world that Pandora liked more than having a good old roll around in mud. In no time at all most of the mud was pummelled flat. The stream began to flow again. Once more, the family home was saved.

The next day, when Mr Jethroe saw this, he was so angry he broke into a hot sweat. This time he made a plan that wouldn't be undone. For the rest of that day, in the sweltering sun, Mr Jethroe built a proper dam made of bricks and cement. By the time it was finished he was exhausted. "And that will be that! Nothing will be able to move this dam." And sadly, he was right.

The Frog family were so upset they were all in tears. They had no idea what to do. As a last resort, Felicity Frog suggested she was going to visit Mrs Jethroe. She announced she would take along some of the flowers that grew around the pond. Perhaps she could appeal to her better nature. And so, she set about making a beautiful bouquet of water lilies, violets, marsh marigolds, forget-me-nots, and topped it off with the most stunning of orchids. She hopped off, and when she arrived, left the flowers on the Jethroe's doorstep.

Later, when she found the flowers, Mrs Jethroe literally screamed in excitement. "Where did these flowers come from!?" Mr Jethroe came to the front door and examined them.

"They look like they come from the pond. I've dried it out so we can make more money growing wheat."

Mrs Jethroe screamed again. This time in alarm. "You can't do that Mr Jethroe. You see this orchid at the top of the bouquet? This flower is one of the rarest in the world! We won't have to grow wheat in that field anymore. If we tell the World-Wide Nature Fund about this, they will help pay to look after the meadow and pond where they grow."

And there we have it. Quite inadvertently, and thanks to the beauty of nature, the Frog Family had saved not only themselves, but all of the beauty, the nature and life that shared the meadow with them. Thankfully nature, the countryside, and most importantly the planet, is worth more than all the money in the world.

Kassandra and the Dressing Up Box

When most children look out the window and see that it's raining it doesn't make them very happy. That's not the case with the girl in this tale. When Kasandra saw it was raining it always made her happy. The rain outside meant she had permission to go into the attic and play with her Great, Great Grandmother's dressing up box.

Very little was known about Kasandra's Great, Great Grandmother. Rumours claimed she was an adventurer who had travelled the world. It was said she had even visited lands and islands that may have been steeped in mystery and magic. Mythical places.

One secret, which Kasandra kept to herself, was that every time she opened her grandmother's dressing up box, she would find a different outfit in it. Was it magic? Quite possibly. Because those outfits always led to an adventure.

On this rainy-day Kassandra opened the box to find shoes with buckles on, a long black coat with golden buttons, and a Tricorn hat with skull and crossbones on the front. She immediately knew what it was, "This is a pirate's costume!"

Once she had dressed herself, Kassandra rubbed her hands excitedly and got ready to leave the attic. Cheerfully, she said out loud to herself, "This is where the adventure begins."

And the adventure did begin indeed! When Kassandra came down from the attic she was no longer in her home. Instead, she emerged on a beautiful sunlit beach.

Just offshore she saw a ship. This ship flew a flag that was the same as her hat, a black flag with skull and crossbones known as The Jolly Roger. In the fashion of a real pirate, she called out, "Ahoy there!"

"Ahoy there!" One of the pirates shouted back.

In no time the ship had welcomed Kassandra aboard. The crew of the ship were very friendly and welcoming. They didn't seem at all like the fearsome pirates of legend. However, Kassandra was yet to meet the ship's captain.

Suddenly, a bell rang. The crew of the ship became very quiet and frightened looking. A pirate introduced himself to Kassandra. His name was Johnny Goldtooth. Probably named because he had a golden tooth. He told her, "Best be quiet now. That bell means the captain is about to come up from below deck. He is the most fearsome of sailors."

And through double doors on the ships deck the captain emerged. Captain Fish-lips was indeed a fearsome looking man. He had a wooden leg, a patch over one eye, and a parrot on his shoulder. The parrot was an amazing creature who could talk. Traditionally pirate's parrots tended to say the same thing over and over. Pieces of eight, pieces of eight, tended to be the most common phrase. But, Captain Fish-lips' parrot was a genuine wonder. It could speak fluent English, and it did so then.

"Listen up crew! The captain is not a happy man today. It has been months since we have captured and plundered another ship for their gold. If we don't have any success today, one of you will be made to walk the plank! SQUAWK!" How amazing, Kassandra thought.

Then the captain spoke, "That's right, ye bunch of sackless seadogs. No gold today and the consequences shall be truly dreadful."

Next to Kassandra, Johnny Goldtooth began to tremble. She asked him, "Why haven't you raided any ships for so long?"

"Because none of us are really pirates!" Johnny wailed, "We got drunk and pressganged into working on this ship. Whenever we go after a ship, we deliberately don't catch it. The captain has been fooled for a while now, but we think he is beginning to suspect!"

Kassandra thought hard to herself. This truly is a genuine conundrum. How can she possibly help the crew? Then she had an idea.

"Excuse me Johnny, but are there any Islands near here?"

"There is mam. I have a map here in my waistcoat."

Kassandra became quite animated, "You have a map! That's exactly what I need."

Next, Kassandra produced a pen from her pocket and marked an X on the map of the Island. She approached the fearsome Captain Fish-Lips, "Captain I have a suggestion. Instead of going to all the trouble of raiding that ship, why don't we follow this map to this island? It has an X on it. I'm sure you know what that means?"

"Ahar! I do indeed, ye young scallywag. That means there be treasure buried on that island. Set sail lads! We're on a mission to find buried treasure." And so, the pirates raised their sails and set off.

Johhny Goldtooth approached Kasandra looking most concerned. "My young friend, what have you done? When we get to that island and Fish-lips finds no treasure he will be most furious. He is bound to punish you in the most terrible of ways."

Kassandra just smiled. "Don't worry about that Johnny. I have a plan. When we are on the beach looking for treasure, you head inland, round up the people of the town, and bring them to us."

"I don't think that will worry the captain," said Johnny. Kassandra just continued to smile.

Surely enough, they arrived on the island and headed to the spot Kassandra had marked on the map. They began to dig... and dig... and dig. After an hour of this the Captain became furious. "What useless sea hag did this map belong to? It is a fake!" Kassandra stepped forward and confessed everything. The captain went purple with temper. "Ye shall be made to walk the plank. Shark food is all ye are now!"

Right at that moment, Johnny arrived on the beach with around twenty of the town folks.

Kassandra stepped forward. "Good people of the island, we have come here today to share with you a marvel. We have a parrot who can speak fluently and perhaps even tell your fortune. To enjoy this amazing feat, we ask that you only need pay one gold coin each."

The parrot knew immediately what Kassandra was up to. It began to speak, "Yes, that's right ladies and gentlemen the girl does tell the truth. Err... I predict a future for this island that will be quite sunny most of the time." The townsfolk were stunned. They soon formed an orderly queue, keen to chat with the wonderous bird.

And that is how captain Fish-lips and his crew stopped being pirates and began to run a very successful carnival. The talking parrot became the star attraction. They sailed from island to island, and finally made a fortune that made them all very happy indeed.

Kassandra was dropped back off on the beach. There on the sand was a ladder that led magically back into the attic. She climbed it and returned the costume to the dressing up box. Now, when she came out of the attic, she was back in her home. Best of all, the rain had stopped and it was time to go out and play.

Maddie and Macie's Magic Metal Detector.

Maddie and Macie were the best of friends. Almost everything they did, they did together. That's what good friends do.

On this day, the day that we meet Madison and Macie, it is a special time. Today is Macie's birthday, and Maddison had bought her the most unexpected and exciting of gifts.

"Happy birthday Macie! I've brought you a present."

Macie could barely contain her excitement. She tore off the brightly coloured wrapping paper. Underneath she found a box; she opened this and pulled out...

Well, she pulled out something. She wasn't sure what this something was. It had a long handle like a broom, at the end of the handle was a metal disc like a plate, and on the handle a dial. The dial had four words on it.

METAL. TREASURE. LOST. MAGIC.

Confused, Macie shrugged her shoulders and asked Maddie, "What is this?"

"It's a metal detector," Maddie laughed. Very excited.

Macie was still confused, "But what does it do? How does it work?"

Maddie set the dial to METAL. Slowly she began to move the metal detector around the room. As it got closer to Macie's pockets it began to make a loud electronic noise.

BARP! BARP! BARP!

Macie put her hands in her pockets and pulled out her keys.

Maddie was super excited by this. "You see, it finds metal things! It found the keys in your pocket! Let's go to the beach and look for treasure!"

Macie thought this a splendid idea. This might just be the best birthday ever. Clapping her hands and hopping from foot to foot she agreed. They set off for the beach.

When they arrived at the beach, they discovered two signs. One sign said, 'Digging Allowed.' The other, 'No Digging Allowed.' Being good and decent girls, who knew that rules are important, they went to work with the metal detector in the area where digging was allowed.

They set the detector's dial to TREASURE. In no time at all the metal detector came to life.

BARP! BARP! BARP!

"Quick," Macie told Maddie. "We've found something. It might be treasure."

Thrilled, they both started digging in the sand where the metal detector made its electronic noise. Could it be treasure? Could it be an entire chest filled with gold? Could it be a suit of armour from days of old? Alas, all they found was a rusty tin can. Never mind. They decided to try another spot. Once again, in almost no time at all, the metal detector went off again.

BARP! BARP! BARP!

Surely this time it must be treasure. Could it be a trumpet… or an antique vase made of silver and decorated with precious jewels? Joyous, they once again set about their dig.

Alas, this time it's just an old spanner. Never mind, the day was still young. Bright eyed and bushy tailed they set off again. All day long.

BARP! BARP! BARP!

BARP! BARP! BARP!

BARP! BARP! BARP!

Sadly, after a few hours, all they had found was more cans, more junk, more scrap, and one coin that was worth so little it wouldn't even buy them some sweets. They were both very tired from all of that digging.

Just as they were about to give up, Macie moved the detector nearer to the sign that said, 'No Digging'. Suddenly, the metal detector went crazy. Twice as loud. Twice as fast.

BARP! BARP! BARP! BARP! BARP! BARP!

"There must be some treasure here!" Macie was very excited. She was almost about to start digging when Maddie stopped her.

"But Macie. You can't dig there. There is a sign, it says no digging!"

But Macie was too eager. She wanted to set right all the disappointing things they had found. She began to dig immediately. As expected, her shovel hit something large and metal. There was a loud CLANG!

"This must be treasure!"

Macie was too excited to notice that a strange rumbling was coming from the ground directly below her...

Maddie had a very concerned look on her face. She was about to warn her when all of a sudden...

WHOOSH!

Macie had hit a water pipe! She was blasted into the air and did two summersaults, a back flip. As quickly as it began, the water ebbed away and she landed softly back on the sand.

Despite being all wet, they both found this very funny... Perhaps they were laughing too soon?

Maddie and Macie agreed that even though they didn't find any treasure, the day had indeed been a splendid adventure. However, they were now both very tired from all of that digging. They decided it was time to get home and put their feet up with a bowl of ice cream.

After a long walk they finally arrived back. Macie put her hand into her pocket to get her keys and unlock the front door. Much to her surprise they weren't there.

"Oh no. My keys must have come out of my pocket when I got blasted into the air by the water!" Macie was so worn out she was close to crying.

"Don't worry Macie," Maddie reassured her, "Look! On the metal detector! We can set it to find things that are LOST!" And right enough Macie remembered. They decided to head back to the beach.

After a bit of searching and a lot of, BARP! BARP! BARP, the keys were found. Hurrah! But now Maddie and Macie were both truly exhausted.

"I'm too tired to walk all the way back Maddie."

"I know. I'm too tired as well!"

And that's when Maddie had the best of ideas. Smiling she turned to Macie, "Wait a minute, isn't there a setting on the metal detector that says magic?"

Macie nodded quickly in agreement, "Yes there is! Maybe that can help get us home."

They reset the dial and in no time the detector was off again.

BARP! BARP! BARP!

They dug up a bicycle wheel.

BARP! BARP! BARP!

They dug up some pedals.

BARP! BARP! BARP!

It's another wheel.

BARP! BARP! BARP!

And now they found a frame.

In no time at all, Maddie and Macie had all the parts needed to assemble a bicycle. And not just any old bicycle, a special type of bicycle, a bicycle made for two! They built a tandem! Now they were able to get home easily. The metal detector was magical after all.

After a cycle home, a large bowl of ice cream was thoroughly enjoyed by both. A splendid adventure indeed.

Team Work Makes the Dream Work.

At the foot of a huge mountain range known as the Peekahoodoos there was a village that went by the name of Longaeval. It was believed that the village got this name because the people who lived there had a peculiar characteristic. Everybody born in Longaeval had incredibly long legs. This was no bad thing. It gave them many advantages. They were tall and could easily harvest fruit in the summer, they could clean the higher windows without the use of a ladder, they could skip and jump much further than regular folks, and best of all they could run really, really fast.

The people of Longaeval loved sports. They were great at them. Long jump, they had it nailed. High jump, even better. But there was one sport that the women of Longaeval loved above all others, and that was the game of hockey. They were so fast they could race from one end of a hockey pitch to the other. With their long legs they could easily outstep one another when an awkward tackle came in. But, despite all this sporting prowess, they had become bored by constantly having draws together when they played each other. They were just too evenly matched.

Hence, it was decided a messenger should be sent out to the other villages on this side of the Peekahoodoo mountains. The messenger took a challenge to them. A tournament could now take place to find out who was truly the best at hockey.

In a few short weeks everything was in place. Six teams came from the other villages. Five of the other villages sent teams that were made up of people who looked just like you and me. You can guess what happened. That's right! The Longaeval women's hockey team beat them all easily. They swerved around them, they outran them, they skipped over tackles, and they scored the most goals.

All seemed fairly inevitable until the villagers from Weesomefolk arrived. Like the ladies of Longaeval the women of Weesomefolk had acquired their name because of a peculiar characteristic. They were all incredibly short.

The women of Longaeval laughed when they saw them, thinking this would be an easy match. However, they were in for a surprise. Yes, it's true that the Longaeval women could outrun and outmanoeuvre them, but that didn't matter. All the Weesomefolk ladies had to do was hang around the Longaeval goal. Whenever the ball came to them, they easily slid it right between the legs of the Longaeval goalkeeper.

By the end of the match, they had won by seventeen goals to three! The Longaevel team were furious.

After the match, their captain Lilly Longshanks called a meeting.

"This has been a terrible humiliation. But how can we ever defeat the women of Weesomefolk? Thanks to their size they have far too much of an advantage against us!"

From the back of the room a player named Lilius Leggerend suggested that she may have an idea. She told the group so, "I have an idea. What if there is a solution to our problem on the other side of the Peekahoodoo mountains?"

On hearing this most of the team scoffed. Nobody had ever climbed over the mountains to see what was on the other side. There might not be anything there at all. For all they knew she might get over them and fall off the edge of the world. But Lilius, in fear of being mocked again, kept secret her secret to herself. Her grandfather had told her legends of the people on the other side of the mountains. She simply informed the rest of them that she had made her decision, and in the morning, she would set off on her quest.

This was no easy task Lilius had set for herself. The mountains were steep, rocky, and treacherous. It was said that at night bears and wolves stalked their valleys. But Lilius was a fearless and determined young woman. Plus, more than anything, she wanted to see her team win at hockey again. With a rucksack full of supplies and some warm winter clothes on she set off on her journey.

Many hours later, when Lilius looked over her shoulder, the village she left behind was a tiny dot on the landscape. Soon she was up to her ankles in snow, and then her knees, and eventually, as she began to get towards the steepest parts of the mountains, the snow came up to her thighs.

The snow was very deep indeed, but Lilius was not put off. Rather than set up camp, she decided to keep on walking throughout the night. Besides, a camp fire may attract unwanted visitors.

All through the night, and into the next day she went. Finally, she came over the peak of the mountains and began to descend to the other side. In the distance she could see a village that looked quite similar in size to the one she had left behind. Eventually, she came to a road sign pointing towards her destination. The sign said, 'Welcome to Broadumbucus.' On seeing the sign, Lilius smiled. She had a feeling that the legends her grandfather had told her might just be true.

On entering the village, Lilius was not too surprised to see that everybody in the village had incredibly long arms.

The people of Broadumbucus also loved sports. They loved tennis, and handball, and volleyball, and anything that involved having the advantage of very long arms. Lilius approached the village elders, and together they formed a plan.

Two days later, Lilius was back in Longaeval. This time she had with her a small party of athletes from Broadumbucus. She called a meeting of the hockey team and told them of her plan. The captain was delighted.

Later that same day, a rematch with Weesomefolk got underway. However, now the Longaeval ladies had a new goalkeeper from Broadumbucus. As much as the Weesomefolk team tried to get the ball past her they just could not. Her long arms stopped almost every shot. The final score was twenty-seven to four in favour of Longaevel. Everyone in the village was delighted.

Viewing all of this were the people from the five other villages. One of these folks was an incredibly smart young woman called Jilly. As backs were being slapped and cheers were dying down Jilly stepped forward with a proposal.

"People of the six villages to the left of the Peekahoodoos, and people from Broadumbucus, I have a proposal. As we can see the solution to winning this game was to mix people of different abilities and leg and arm length. Can you imagine what would happen if we mixed an entire team? We could have some long legs, some long arms, some short people, and some regular folks. Together that might make us the best team in the all of the land."

And Jilly was right. By combining all these different advantages, and some may say disadvantages, together as a whole they were unstoppable. Because being the best isn't about one shape or another. It's about playing as a team and combining all the types we can find. As many as possible... Together.

Phillis and her Magic Phone.

Of all the girls in the science class Phillis was by far the smartest. Some teachers felt she may even be a genius. Despite this, Phillis came from an ordinary family who would often struggle to make ends meet. Both her mother and father worked three jobs each, and sometimes they struggled with heating bills. Occasionally they had to resort to getting help from a local foodbank. Although Phillis knew this was nothing to be ashamed of, she sometimes felt embarrassed by their situation. Other girls could also be cruel to Phillis and taunt her about being poor.

One day in biological chemistry class Phillis was studying chameleons. Chameleons are amazing creatures who can change colour to blend in with their backgrounds. It was whilst studying them that she was struck with an idea.

Mr Boffins the science teacher had supplied the class with some chameleon skin for them to examine. Don't worry, no chameleons were hurt in the process. He had gathered the skin from his pet chameleon Nobby, who liked to shed it and grow a new one every few months.

Phillis had an idea. She took a sample of the skin, mixed it with some magnesium, added a splash of something secret, and created a crystal. She then took this crystal and placed it inside the lens of the camera in her phone.

Phillis was well aware, as we all are, that people like to use filters on their phones when using the camera. These filters can do all sorts of things, but mainly they are designed to make us look better, if not a little unnatural.

At school the next day she approached a girl named Lesley. Lesley had red hair and was covered in freckles. Although Phillis thought Lesley looked great, she was aware that Lesley was always unhappy about her freckles.

"Lesley, I have a proposal for you. If I take a photo of you with the magic filter in my phone, I can make your freckles disappear." Lesley thought she was just making stuff up and told Phillis to go away. But Phillis persevered and persuaded Lesley to have her photo taken. Once she had her snap, she went into the app she had created, and with a swipe of her finger removed the freckles from Lesley's photograph. And behold, the exact same thing happened to Lesley's face!

She was over the moon and quickly ran off to tell the rest of the school about Phillis's amazing invention. In no time at all word was out and a queue had formed. Everybody demanded that Phillis fix various characteristics of their faces.

Click and swipe, teeth got straightened. Click again, and ears got smaller. Click once more, and hair was changed from black to blond. All day long Phillis was able to grant the children at school their wish of looking slightly better, even though she thought they all looked fine in the first place.

Soon, word spread across the land and Phillis began to charge money for the use of her amazing phone and app. Within a couple of months, she had amassed a fortune. Her parents were finally able to get some rest. They all moved into a large mansion in the countryside. Everything seemed perfect.

Now that Phillis was famous, news had got out to the rich and powerful. One day she was summoned to see the Prime Minister and to bring her phone with her.

The PM wasn't the most cheerful of women. Most thought it was the stress of the job. However, the truth was sadder than that. The Prime Minister had a daughter who suffered terribly from constant sadness. Nobody knew why she was so sad all the time, but a good guess would say it was because her mother was always far too busy to spend and quality time with her.

The PM had an election coming up in a few months and she wanted to look her best for the campaign. And so, she asked Phillis to use her phone and app to remove all the wrinkles from her face. Phillis thought this to be a fairly straightforward task. She took her snap and then on the filter began to smooth over the wrinkles in the PM's features. She made her picture look as smooth as a polished stone, like the ones you find on the beach. But, when Phillis looked up from her work, she saw the most alarming sight. The PM was completely featureless. She had overdone things! Her mouth was a slot, her nose was flat and her face had taken on the shape and flatness of a wooden spoon.

"Change me back!" The Prime Minister shrieked, "I can't go around looking like this. How will anybody know what I am feeling like? I can't smile, I can't even express any emotions!"

"I don't know how," Phillis pleaded, "I've only ever got it to work one way. I don't know how to get it to reverse things."

The Prime Minister was furious and had Phillis and her parents locked in a laboratory until a solution could be found. Their fortune was taken away and their mansion sold off to the highest bidder. They were once again back on the skids.

Phillis worked tirelessly. It turned out the answer was staring her in the face. Eventually she figured out that if she reversed the camera on her phone, she could change faces, and next change them back again. She was hugely relieved.

Once again, she found herself before the PM. She explained how the phone could now work both ways, and undid the smoothness on her face. The PM shrieked with pleasure.

Just as this was happening the Prime Ministers daughter came down from her bedroom to see what all the commotion was about.

The PM always felt sad on seeing her unhappy daughter. If only she knew a way to cheer her up. That's when she had an idea.

"So, Phillis, you say you can now reverse the effects of the phone? That means there's no danger of me being stuck with a face I don't want?"

"Yes Prime Minister, you can change forwards and back."

With that the PM took the phone from Phillis and set the app so that it added puppy ears and a rabbit's nose to her face. With a quick click her real face was transformed. She quickly turned to her daughter.

"I say precious, what do you think of my new look?"

And something truly remarkable began to happen. First her daughter smiled, and then her shoulders began to shake as she giggled, finally she was clutching her sides laughing.

This went on all day. The PM constantly undoing and then adding more ridiculous filters to her face. She was only limited by her imagination. Phillis was so relieved she gave her the phone; she could always make another.

Once again Phillis and her family were free, but with no phone her fortune was gone. Luckily news of her talents had reached the space agency NASA.

The scientists at NASA had come up with a stunning idea regarding how to use Phillis's invention. They positioned a satellite above earth with one of her special crystals inside a telescopic camera. Next, they pointed it back at earth. With a click, wherever there was a drought, the satellite could make it rain, wherever there was a forest fire, the satellite could erase it. And so on and so on. Technology has a tendency to start small and later think big. In the end Phillis became NASA's chief scientific advisor. Magic phone apps were just the beginning.

The Girl Who Loved Yellow.

Once upon a time, there was a magical land made up of the most spectacular colours. It was a land so beautiful that almost everyone who lived there was happy.

This land had a name, and its name was Vivid Whereabouts. In Vivid Whereabouts, if something was red then it was the warmest of reds. Squirrels, tulips, poppies, and foxes were all of the most breathtakingly red. Things that were green were the freshest of greens. Emeralds, frogs, apples, and grass were all of the most glorious of greens. And so on...

But there was one colour, and one girl, who really stood out. A girl whom everyone loved in the land of Vivid Whereabouts. Her name was Yamilet, and she was the girl who loved yellow. Yamilet had beautiful yellow hair, her raincoat and wellingtons were always yellow, even her eyes were like yellow dandelions.

There was one thing that Yamilet loved to do and that was to make other people happy. Everybody called her their little ray of yellow sunshine. She made the finest golden honey from bees that were yellow. She grew bananas that were yellow and shared them with others at school. She played beautiful melodies on her yellow trumpet. She had yellow pet canaries that would join in and sing along to her marvellous music. Wherever Yamilet, the girl who loved yellow went, people were glad to see her... Well, almost everyone. Like many lands that we find, Vivid Whereabouts was ruled over by a queen.

Queen Beatrice Babage was her name, and despite all of her wealth, her fame, and her power, she was an angry and jealous ruler of the land of Vivid Whereabouts.

You see, queen Beatrice Babage didn't like bright colours. The reasons for this were largely unknown. Rumour was she was just an unhappy sourpuss.

It's with Queen Beatrice and Yamilet that our tale takes an unfortunate turn. In one way or another Yamilet had helped or made happy many, many people in the land of Vivid Whereabouts. And so, one bright sunny day, Yamilet took it upon herself to cheer up the queen.

In her typical considerate way, she prepared for the Queen a fantastic surprise. In a yellow basket she gathered some honey, some bananas, a yellow rubber duck, and a beautiful bouquet of yellow flowers. They were of the most glorious of yellows and included daffodils, sunflowers and marigolds. All together the basket was the most radiant looking of gifts.

And so, Yamilet set off to visit the queen.

On arrival at the queen's home Yamilet made her way over the moat and pushed open two huge black doors that led into the castle itself. As she made her way through the corridors there was one thing Yamilet noticed... There were no bright colours. The décor was made up of dark blues, blacks and greys. How peculiar.

Eventually Yamilet entered a large room, and there asleep on her throne was the Queen. Yamilet approached her and gently shook her awake.

"Queen Beatrice, I've brought you a present. I thought it may help you feel happy."

When the queen opened her eyes, Yamilet was given the most startling of frights. She glared at her basket of beautiful yellow things and screamed.

"Aaaaaaarrrrgggggghhhhhh! I hate yellow things! Get out! You shall be punished for this. Punished in ways most dreadful."

Yamilet fled the castle as quick as she could. How could anybody possibly not like yellow things? They're so bright and cheerful?

Now the queen set about hatching the most wicked of plans. Like many queens in many lands, queen Beatrice Babage employed a wizard. She set him to cast the most wicked of spells.

When the people of Vivid Whereabouts woke the next day, they were shocked to find that the land and everything in it was now coloured dark blue, black and grey. Red Foxes tails were now no longer warm, green apples were grey and no longer delicious to look at.

But... Queen Beatrice Babage had saved the worst spell of all for kindly Yamilet. On that day Yamilet was brushing her hair and looking in the mirror. Her skin, her teeth, her lips and all the rest of her began to turn yellow! She shrieked and turned away from the mirror. Now she discovered that everything she looked at turned yellow. Her cat turned yellow, her parents turned yellow, the furniture, the curtains, all of it yellow! Even for Yamilet this was too much!

However, there was one thing the Queen didn't bargain on. The sun in the sky was no longer yellow. The sun was now grey. No warmth, no sunshine and no crops can be grown from the colour grey. That's why the sun is yellow. It's there to keep us warm and happy and fed.

Soon the people of Vivid Whereabouts grew very angry. A mob marched towards the castle.

When they arrived, the people demanded to see the queen or they would burn the castle to the ground. But the queen refused to come out. Just as things were about to become troublesome a man at the back of the crowd shouted. "Look! Look! A path of yellow is coming towards us!"

And there was Yamilet. As she made her way through the countryside, everything she looked at turned yellow.

"Yamilet! You can save us. You can save the crops. You can save the weather."

And Yamilet knew what they wanted her to do. For a few seconds Yamilet looked at the grey sun and slowly it began to turn yellow again. The sun's warmth and radiant glow once again began to be felt across Vivid Whereabouts.

The people were delighted, but they also now knew of Yamilet's plight. Angry, they demanded to see the Queen. They demanded her wizard lift his spells.

Frightened of what may happen, the Queen hastily consulted her wizard and the spells were lifted. The colour returned to Vivid Whereabouts and Yamilet no longer saw yellow wherever she looked.

Yamilet was not only kind but also forgiving. She asked the queen why she so disliked bright colours. And here's the surprise. The queen did like colours... But her eyes did not. They were sensitive to sunshine and bright things.

"I can fix that!" Yamilet cried. And she presented the Queen with a pair of yellow tinted sunglasses.

And for the first time ever queen Beatrice Babage could enjoy colours. Just a little less vibrant than folks were used to.

The Magical Gramophone.

Wynter and Wanda were two sisters who loved to explore. One place they particularly enjoyed visiting was an old junk shop, situated in the narrow lanes of their local town.

The shop was owned by an elderly Japanese gentleman named Mr Tachibana. He was always pleased to see the girls, as he was a gentleman who encouraged the adventurous spirit.

When the girls arrived that day Mr Tachibana greeted them with a warm smile and told them he had something special to show them. He led them through to a curtained off area of his store where there was a large unusual shaped object with a cloth over it. When he removed the cloth underneath was an old gramophone. It had a square box body for playing records upon and a horn that protruded out of the top which amplified the music it could play. On the side of the box was a turn crank handle for winding the gramophone up to make it work.

Wynter and Wanda had never seen anything like it before.

"What is it?" asked Wynter.

"It's a gramophone player," Mr Tachibana told them, "It's like a record player, but much older. They say this one comes from an ancient part of Japan and has magical powers."

Both the girls laughed at this. Mr Tachibana was always telling them that he had magical objects in his junk shop. More often than not they suspected he was just trying to humour them.

Mr Tachibana made them an offer, "I'll tell you what, I have to leave the shop for an hour to go on an errand to the bank. You can stay here and play with this if you want. I also have some old records that came with it. You simply put the record on the turntable and off you go. But, one little word of warning. These records are also magic. So, pay attention to which ones you choose to play." The girls laughed at this again.

"That sounds like a great idea Mr Tachibana. We'll watch the shop for you while you're away," Wanda said, humouring him. Mr Tachibana smiled and bowed in the traditional Japanese way of saying thank you. "All you have to do is put a record on, close your eyes, and when you open them again the fun will begin." Then he left for the bank.

Wynter picked through some off the records on the floor. She selected one with a picture of the Amazon Jungle on it. Above the photograph on the sleeve were the words, 'Sounds of The Jungle'.

She turned the crank handle, placed the record on the turntable, and then she and Wanda took a seat on a nearby old battered sofa. Next, they closed their eyes.

Soon enough, the room was filled with the sounds of chirruping insects, squawking parrots, chattering monkeys and the rustle of many animals making their way through the thick jungle foliage.

"That's amazing." The sounds made Wanda's skin tingle. Only, it wasn't just the sounds. Wanda was sure she could feel a small breeze and a heavy humidity beginning to fill the room. When they both opened their eyes, their breath was taken away. They were in the middle of the Amazon Jungle.

"Wow! It is magic!" Cried Wynter, leaping up from the battered old sofa, "We should go exploring!"

Although Wanda liked the idea of this very much, she also felt a little cautious. "But what if there are animals out there that are dangerous? Things like snakes or gorillas?"

And no sooner had Wynter said this than they heard something large move in the tall grass just behind them.

"What was that?" Wanda pointed, "There's something large in the tall grass. But I can't see anything."

The reason they couldn't make anything out was because this particular animal had perfect camouflage that kept it hidden. It was an animal with stripes and large teeth. It let out a momentous roar.

"It's a tiger! Wynter takes the record back off. I think we're about to be eaten!"

Wynter leapt at the gramophone and removed the record. With a whoosh and pop, they were back in the junk shop.

"Wow. That was scary. But also, fun! Let's play another!" Despite the close shave Wanda was still very excited. Wynter was too.

They returned to the records and Wynter picked up one with a photo of some racing cars on the front. "Let's try this one," she said.

They both settled back into the sofa and closed their eyes. The next thing they felt was the wind whooshing very fast through their hair. They could hear the sound of roaring engines. When they opened their eyes, they both looked down to find they were still on the sofa. "It hasn't worked," Wanda said. Wynter hurriedly replied, "Oh yes it has! Look up!"

Wanda did so, and was amazed to see the sofa was hurtling around a racing track. They were going incredibly fast and overtaking the racing cars. "We're going to win the race!" shouted Wynter, above the roaring noise.

Just as they were approaching the finish line there was a loud CLICK! Suddenly they were back at the start of the race. Whoosh, they went around again, and once more, just as they were about to cross the finish line, CLICK! Once again, they were back at the start.

"I know what's wrong," Wynter told Wanda, "The record is stuck. We keep jumping back to the start when the needle on the gramophone does. Look to the side of the track, just before the finish line, I can see the gramophone. This time when we pass, stick out your leg and give it a thump!"

Wanda did exactly that and they went over the finish line first. The record came to an end and with a whoosh and a pop they were back in the junk shop.

Excited, they returned to the records on the floor. This time Wanda picked up one that had a frightening looking old house on the front. In the window off the house, they could see the silhouette of a woman, or was it... a ghost? They both looked at each other nervously. Suddenly, they heard the bell to Mr Tachibana's shop ring. He had returned from the bank.

"Hello girls did you enjoy the gramophone?"

Wynter and Wanda could hardly contain themselves and both spoke hurriedly, trying to explain their adventure.

"We were in the jungle... it was all noisy... and warm and humid, and then there was a tiger!" Gasped Wynter.

"And then we were in a race, although not in a car but on the sofa, but we kept going back to the beginning, until we thumped the gramophone and won!" Wanda explained.

Mr Tachibana laughed heartily, "Why you girls have an imagination that's even more vivid than mine. What record were you going to play next?"

Wanda held up the scary looking record with the house on the front. "This one."

"Oh! I would suggest with an imagination as colourful as yours you leave that for another day. Sounds like you've had a fair old adventure already."

Wynter and Wanda couldn't agree more. And they all laughed together.

The Queen of the Moon.

If there was one food that Charlotte loved more than any other it was to nibble on a nice bit of cheese. She loved them all, because there were so many to choose from. Brie, Camembert, Cottage, Cream, Monterey Jack, Mozzarella, Romano, and Ricotta were just a few among the many she loved.

However, one thing Charlotte was forbidden to do was to eat cheese after 6pm. Her mother warned her that if she did so she may have strange dreams that would unsettle her sleeping.

One summer evening, the type where the moon rises and there is still light in the sky, Charlotte sat gazing upwards. Doesn't the moon look like it is made of cheese? She thought to herself. She jumped up and down with her butterfly net, pretending to catch the moon within it. If only I could catch the moon. What a cheese feast that might be.

Not too long after this Charlotte's mother called her into the house. It was time for bed.

As Charlotte got ready for bed, she accidentally dropped her hairband on the floor. As she bent over to pick it up, she noticed something under her bed, it was a half-eaten cheese sandwich that she had meant to have earlier. She had forgotten when she went out to play.

Oh what harm can it cause, she thought, and had a quick nibble.

Once into bed, inevitably, just like her mother had warned, she began to dream.

Charlotte found herself back outside looking at the moon. She knew she was dreaming and yet this dream felt particularly vivid and real. I wonder if I can reach it in my dream?

Suddenly, standing beside Charlotte was a beautiful and elegant woman. She wore a gown of silver silk and her head was topped with a long-pointed crown that looked like it was made of stalagmites that you find in some caves.

"Who are you?" Charlotte asked politely.

"I'm the Queen of the Moon." Replied the woman.

"I've always wanted to go there," gushed Charlotte, "I've heard it's made of cheese!"

"And now you can. Look behind you."

When Charlotte turned around, she saw a huge telescope. The Queen told her to look into it. When she did the moon looked much closer.

"Now if we both climb inside and walk to the other end, we can reach the moon."

Charlotte was stunned to be told this, but did as she was advised. Sure enough, after a short walk through the inside of the telescope, they emerged out the other end and stepped onto the surface of the moon.

Charlotte bent down and scooped up a handful of the moon. It felt soft and creamy. She gave the moon-stuff a sniff. "It smells like cheese!"

"That's because it is. However, Charlotte you must not eat too much of it, you must only have a nibble."

Charlotte wasn't too impressed on hearing this. "But why? It smells so delicious."

The Queen of the moon told Charlotte that each night, whilst everyone was in bed, a great dragon would visit the moon and eat his fill. Despite this, the moon could eventually grow back to its full size. This is the reason why sometimes when you look at the moon it is only a sliver of a crescent and sometimes a full circle.

"And now I am going to leave you here to play for a while," the Queen told Charlotte, "I have some important business to attend to with the Queen of the Sun. She hates to be kept waiting and made late for her rise."

Once the Queen had glided off Charlotte had a fantastic time. She could leap great heights because gravity is much lighter on the moon. Soon she developed a game of leaping into the moon's many craters. She would disappear inside for a second and then pop, she would come bounding out of another hole on a different part of the white surface.

After a while of this, all the jumping around began to make Charlotte very hungry indeed. "I'll just have a little nibble." She scooped a handful of moon cheese. It was so delicious. She couldn't help herself but have some more... and some more... and then even more. After eating so much, she nodded off, tired from having had her fill.

Charlotte wasn't sure how long she had been asleep, but she was suddenly woken by a roaring and terrible voice, "Who has been eating my fill of the moon?"

When Charlotte sat up, there above her was a great silver Dragon with eyes the colour of shiny silver stars.

"I only had a little," she protested.

"You have eaten far too much of the moon! Now when I have my fill, I will have to eat all that is left of the moon. There will never be a moon in the sky again."

With that, the dragon began to take huge bites out of the moon. One bite and the moon was at three quarters, another and the moon was at half, one more and soon it would be a sliver of a crescent.

Suddenly, up from a crater popped the Queen of the Moon. Beside her was another woman. She wore a dress of golden silk and halo of bright light shone around her head. This was the Queen of the Sun. She stepped forward and spoke to the dragon, "Great Moon Dragon, we are most apologetic that you cannot have your full fill of the moon tonight. I am the Queen of the Sun. I'll bet you've never tasted how delicious the sun is?"

The dragon considered this for a moment. He spoke, "I have not. Is it as delicious as the moon?"

"Twice as much. It is as sweet as honey and three times as soft and runny," the Sun Queen told him, "If you stop eating now, I shall bring the sun up and you can have your fill."

The dragon accepted these terms gleefully. As the sun began to rise the dragon flew toward it. Of course, as we all know, the sun is nothing like the moon. But the dragon did not know that the Sun Queen had fooled him. The dragon landed on the surface of the sun and was immediately disintegrated into a frazzle. The moon would be safe again.

"Time for you to get back home." The Moon Queen told Charlotte. After all of this Charlotte was very keen to get back to bed.

The Moon Queen snapped a stalagmite from her crown and waved it like a wand, "Now sleep..."

When Charlotte woke up, she was back in bed. As fun as her dream had been it had also been a little frightening. Next time if she fancied a nibble before bed, she decided she would have a nice stick of celery. That seemed like a much safer bet.

Zamira's Bonkers Botany Set.

If there's one thing, we can all agree about, it is that mother nature makes our planet look truly beautiful. All the trees, the green, the flowers, and leafy plants make up the most magnificent of sights. Even in the desert you can find exotic looking cacti that have adapted to a life in the hot sun. Even they grow into the most magnificent of shapes.

Zamira was a girl who loved plants so much her mother often called her mother nature's child.

One Saturday afternoon, when they were both visiting the local shopping centre, Zamira spotted something in a shop window that made her jump with excitement.

"Look mum! It's a botany set!" For those that don't know, a botany set is a kit for growing, fertilising, and producing magnificent flowers and plants.

As it was close to Zamira's birthday, her mother told her she could have this gift early. As long as she was careful and followed to the letter all the instructions inside. Zamira promised that she would.

When they got home, as it was a gorgeous sunny day, Zamira decided to take her Botany set into the garden.

Inside it were samples of leaves, stem, bark, flowers, seeds and fruits. Along with the plant life came a variety of fertilisers, chemicals and powders, that if used correctly, would help her grow plants. They all had a warning sticker on them that said, 'Do not mix! Remove from the box one at a time!'

This is where the trouble began. Zamira was so excited and so passionate about growing some new and exotic plants that she took everything out of the box all at once. She placed them on a table in front of her. Next, she put some soil in a little pot and popped some seeds in.

As she was doing this, what Zamira wasn't aware of, was a large crow sitting in the tree branches above her. He was greedily eyeing up some of the seed packets she had pulled from her set.

Whoosh! The crow swept down and began to peck at the seeds. Zamira was furious and flapped him away with her hands. As she did this, many of the chemicals and fertilisers got mixed together. The crow returned to his branch. Angrily still eyeing up his dinner.

Zamira surveyed the mess that had been made. "Oh well, I suppose it won't matter too much. I mean, all of this stuff does the same job. It's all meant to help plants grow." And with that thought she tried to sort things out.

She arranged some more pots and planted more seeds. The surprises began when she started to add the mixed-up chemicals.

With a dropper she added some mixture to her pot, and much to her surprise, a shoot immediately sprouted. "Wow that was quick!" She added some more drops and a green leafy vine grew in-front of her so fast it now tottered slightly above her head. "This is amazing! I wonder what happens if I add this potion." And with that thought, Zamira broke every rule that the instructions had advised her against.

She now turned to a different pot and added a different mixture. POP! Just like that a cactus shot up. It had the most fearsome looking spikes and a strange red and white flower on the top. The flower made the cactus almost look as if it had a mouth and was smiling.

"I think I've invented a new type of plant. I wonder what happens when I add some of this stuff?" Zamira added even more mixes and compounds. At first nothing happened. She felt a little disappointed. But then… Did that cactus wobble slightly? It seemed to tremble for a moment? Perhaps it's trying to grow some more? She added more mixture. That's when things got a little out of hand.

The cactus trembled once more and then the flower that looked like a mouth grinned and spoke. It no longer just looked like a mouth, it was one!

"Hello Zamira. Very pleased to meet you." Zamira jumped back startled. This can't be right, she thought. Plants shouldn't talk. "Err… Pleased to meet you. Is there… err… anything I can get you?"

"Yes please," replied the smiling cactus, "I'd like a knife and fork thank you. I'm very hungry and I've decided I'm going to eat you all up!" Suddenly roots like feet began to burst out of the plant pot and the cactus slowly lumbered towards Zamira.

Thankfully Zamira was smart. She membered the potion that had made the first plant grow so fast. She emptied an entire bottle into its pot and grabbed a hold. The vine shot up, up into the air with Zamira clinging on. In no time at all she was above the clouds. But far below the cactus had begun to climb. "I'm coming to eat you all up Zamira!"

The next thing that happened was quite unexpected. The crow from earlier landed on the vine next to where Zamira was holding on. He was a very large crow and Zamira was a very slightly built girl. She had an idea. In her pocket were some of the seeds from earlier. She fed these to the crow. He was delighted with the feast. Next Zamira grabbed the large crow by the feet. He seemed to know what she wanted, and with some very heavy flaps of his wings, he took her below the clouds and settled her back on the ground. The cactus had missed all of this and continued to climb to the top of the vine.

Zamira went back into her botany set and found a small tree saw. She began to cut at the bottom of the vine. Saw, saw, saw... Timber! The vine came toppling down and the cactus smashed into a hundred pieces. It was once again just a normal cactus. Lessons had to be learned.

When Zamira got older, she went on to become a famous botanist. She studied how to grow crops in places of the planet where it was difficult to do so. Her work helped many people. One thing she never did was disobey botany instructions ever again. Mother nature has ways of making us pay if we do.

A Silly Story. With a Silly Ending. That Only Ever Scares Grown Ups.

Everybody knows that ghosts aren't real. At least children do. Mums and dads maybe not so much. Gillian was a young girl who wasn't afraid of such things. She knew there is nothing really scary in this world outside our own imaginations.

That's why, on a fateful snowy evening, when hitchhiking with her dad, she was glad she was there to reassure him. He got himself in a right muddle when he thought he was in a haunted wood. But there's no such thing as haunted woods, is there? Gillian knew this. Her dad however.... Well, let's go back to the beginning.

Winter is a strange time to go camping for most, but not for Gillian and her dad. Both of them were adventurers and loved nothing more than the challenges that wild weather and nature can bring. For this camping trip they had decided to visit the Highlands of Scotland. Scotland is a mysterious land filled with legends of days of yore. That means a long time ago.

One thing the Highlands is famous for is the weather can change quite unexpectedly. Gillian and her dad were fully prepared for this. They had all the right gear, were wrapped up super warm, and were actually hoping they might see some snow. Bring it on, they thought. And typical of Scottish weather the clouds did indeed bring it on, only much more ferociously than her dad was expecting. In no time at all they were lost in a blizzard. Gillian's dad got out his map and tried to find their bearings.

"There are two roads forward Gillian. One leads into the hills, so that's no good, the weather will be even worse up there... and this other one leads to... Ooh err."

"What is it dad?"

"Err... it says, this other road leads to something called skeleton woods. I don't like the sound of that!"

Gillian couldn't stop laughing. Her dad was such a scaredy-cat. "There's no such thing as skeletons dad. We'll have to go that way; we'll be able to get some shelter in the trees."

"Are you sure? Ooh err..."

Gillian laughed again, took him by the hand and began marching him confidently towards the woods. Ten minutes later they were on the edge of a large set of trees.

"Ooh, err... Gillian. I'm really not sure about this..."

"Oh come on dad. Don't be such a dafty. There's nothing to be afraid of." And she laughed and laughed.

Suddenly, from behind them both, they saw a light approaching through the blizzard. It was moving quite slowly, coming along the road that they were on.

Gillians dad's mood became much brighter. He turned to her and said, "I think it's a car. We can hitch a lift. I'd much prefer going through these woods safe inside a car than on foot."

"Fair enough dad." They both stuck out their thumbs to hitch a lift.

The car emerged through the blinding and whirling snow. It was a very old car. This was a car that you don't see around so much these days, a very expensive vehicle known as a Rolls Royce Phantom.

"Wow that looks amazing." Gillian cried.

"Ooh err... It looks kind of spooky to me." Gillian's dad was such a silly worrier.

The car slowly came up beside them, it didn't quite stop, but was trundling along slow enough that Gillian's dad was able to open the back door, and they both leaped inside and onto the back seat. Gillian's dad couldn't have been happier.

He swept away the snow that was covering them both, and looking down, began to put their bags on the floor of this antique and special car.

"Oh, thanks so much for picking us up. I err... I was, err... Well, I was just worried my daughter might get frightened in the woods."

"Oh, dad you're such a fibber."

Then Gillian's dad bent up from the floor. When he looked into the front seats he let out a scream. There was nobody driving the car.

"Aaaaaaarghhhh! Gillian. What's this!"

"Oh wow dad. I think we've stepped inside a magic car!"

"A magic car? A magic car?! Gillian it's a haunted car!"

"Oh, don't be so daft dad. This could be amazing."

But Gillian's dad was having none of this. Franticly he tried to pull open the door. No such luck. It had become frozen shut. He tried the other door. Same again, they were trapped. He thought he might faint. He probably would have if Gillian hadn't been having so much fun. However, soon they both had a reason to worry.

As they trundled along, they saw a sign at the side of the road, it said 'Cliff dead ahead. Turn left!' Even Gillian became a little worried at this.

"Oh no dad. With nobody driving we might go over the edge!" Still the car trundled on. In the distance they could both see where a bend in the road began. Still, they went straight towards what could only be the cliffs edge.

Just as they were about to reach a huge fall something truly mystical happened. The window next to the steering wheel opened. In from outside came a withered and ghostly looking old hand. It grabbed the steering wheel and slowly, steadily guided the Rolls Royce Phantom around the bend and out of harm's way.

"Wow!" said Gillian, "I told you dad, it's a magic car." Gillians dad had gone almost as white as the hand that came through the window. Gillian was absolutely loving this adventure. Her dad... perhaps not so much.

Next thing they knew they saw another sign. This one said, 'Warning. Cliff Dead Ahead. Turn right'

"Oh not again!" Wailed Gillian's dad.

Once again, just as they were approaching the bend, the same thing happened. In through the window came the same old withered and ghostly looking hand. Again, it grabbed the steering wheel and guided them to safety.

"I can't take much more of this." Wailed Gillian's dad.

"No need to be afraid dad. The car is obviously protecting us. It's a magic car. I told you it was!"

After what felt like a very long time (At least it felt that way to Gillian's dad) the car slowly ground to a halt. Suddenly the door sprang open and they were both able to get out. Gillian's dad couldn't do so quick enough. He grabbed her by the hand, and with a leap they were back on the road. A voice came from behind them.

"Are you alright?" Gillians dad screamed. There at the back of the car stood a frail looking old man.

"Yes, we're fine," said Gillian. "I think we've just had a trip in a magic car." Then she explained to the old man everything that had happened.

The old man began to laugh, and laugh, and laugh. He could hardly stand up. Eventually he regained control of his faculties.

"You silly sausages," he said, "This isn't a magic or even a haunted car! I've been pushing it for the last three miles. It broke down in the snow."

And with that Gillian's dad finally fainted.

Disclaimer

This book contains opinions and ideas of the author and is meant to teach the reader informative and helpful knowledge while due care should be taken by the user in the application of the information provided. The instructions and strategies are possibly not right for every reader and there is no guarantee that they work for everyone. Using this book and implementing the information/recipes therein contained is explicitly your own responsibility and risk. This work with all its contents, does not guarantee correctness, completion, quality or correctness of the provided information. Misinformation or misprints cannot be completely eliminated.

Printed in Great Britain
by Amazon

81460535R00048